Born in Germany, Ute Maria lived in Eastern Canada, the USA and then Western Canada where she met her British husband. In 1978 they moved outside Cambridge where she taught languages at a private school before becoming Head of Department. She also organised student trips to Russia, Egypt, Turkey, Germany, New York, Washington D.C and Kenya and travelled all over the world in the holidays.

Ute Maria has written short stories, novels, plays and also for children. Now she volunteers for her local primary school where Max continues his journeys to Mars, Jupiter and Saturn.

Max's Marvellous Journey
To the Moon

UTE MARIA SPROULLE

Max's Marvellous Journey
to the Moon

To maisie
with best wishes
from
mrs. Sproulle

Nightingale Books

NIGHTINGALE PAPERBACK

© Copyright 2016
Ute Maria Sproulle

A CIP catalogue record for this title is
available from the British Library.

ISBN: 9781907553762

Nightingale Books is an imprint of
Pegasus Elliot Mackenzie Publishers Ltd.
www.pegasuspublishers.com

First Published in 2016

Nightingale Books
Sheraton House Castle Park
Cambridge England

Printed & Bound in Great Britain

Dedication

To Richard for all his support.

Acknowledgements

To the children, including Catherine, Rosanna, Edmund, Yannick, Kathryn, Krystina, who seventeen years ago first liked this story. To all the nieces and nephews in between, and to today's children, especially Beech Class, who still like it!

1

A Great Idea

Max sat at his bedroom window and stared out at the Moon.

"I wish I was there", he said, "where no one would bother me."

His parents were always telling him to tidy up his room and do his homework and be nice to his aunt, uncle, and cousins and to eat his beans.

He hated beans – and his aunt Minnie would pinch his cheek and say, "my, hasn't he grown!"
His uncle Herb would throw a football at him and say, "catch!", knowing Max would miss it. His cousins teased him. And he was always doing homework!

And he liked his room messy!

"I wish I was on the Moon," he sighed.

"Max, dear, what are you still doing up?" asked his mother as she looked into his room.

"It's late. You should be in bed."

"I was just looking at the Moon," said Max grumpily.

"Did you see the Man in the Moon?" asked his mother coming over to look out of the window with him.

"What Man in the Moon?"

"Well, if you look closely, you can see a face. See, there are the eyes on top, then a long nose, and at the bottom there's a mouth. That's the Man in the Moon."

Max looked very hard and his mother was right. It really looked like there was a man's face on the surface of the Moon!

After his mother had turned out the light, Max lay awake thinking. Wouldn't it be interesting to go and see the Man in the Moon. But how would he do it?

"I know! I'll go and see Professor Boggle. He's always inventing weird things. He'll be able to build me a rocket and then I'll fly to the Moon!"

The next day after school Max went to see the Professor. He lived down the street in a big spooky house. All the kids were scared to go near it because they said it was haunted. But it wasn't haunted, just full of funny machines that hummed and whistled and gurgled and grumped.

Max liked going to see Professor Boggle who, in addition to being an amazing inventor, was also his mother's uncle and she would always send along some cake. Then they would have tea parties with his talking cat, Humphrey, and the Professor would show Max his latest inventions. It was always something strange and wonderful, like an automated lawn mower which cut the grass all by itself, or a robot which took out the rubbish.

Sometimes the inventions wouldn't quite behave the way the Professor wanted them to, like the time the rubbish robot took Humphrey out to the bin and dumped him in it. Humphrey sulked for weeks afterwards and wouldn't speak to anyone. Or the first time the Professor tried out his automated lawnmower. It kept going all the way down the street mowing anything that looked or felt like grass including Mrs. Wilson's woolly green jumper which had fallen off the clothesline. It was a mess! The Professor tried to knit it again on his automated knitting machine but it looked like a big green tent so Max's mother had to buy Mrs. Wilson a new one.

His dad said Professor Boggle should be locked up but his mother had a soft spot for her strange uncle and liked Max to visit him. The Professor had been a famous scientist but now that he was retired nobody wanted to know about his ideas or inventions anymore.

Professor Boggle had once told Max that he had always wanted to be an astronaut, so if anyone could get him to the Moon, the Professor could.

The next day, after school, Max set off with a triple chocolate cake. Humphrey was sunning himself on the porch when he arrived.

"He's inside," he grumbled, for Humphrey was a grumpy cat. "Don't go in."

"Okay," said Max, who was used to Humphrey's ways, and went in anyway.

The Professor was working in the laboratory trying to rev up an engine, which went, *splutter, splutter, burp, ahhhh, pop.*

"Hello, it's me," said Max, peeking around the door. "What's that?"

"Oh, Max, hello! Come and see this! I've just finished my double wombooley infinity drive. Once I've refined it, it will get you from here to – well, to Jupiter," said the Professor excitedly.

"If it works," said Humphrey, slouching in.

"Oh great!" said Max. "That's what I wanted to talk to you about. I want to go to the Moon."

"To the Moon? Wonderful!" said the Professor. "I've always wanted to go to the Moon. A marvellous place. I even worked out a plan a long time ago. Now, where did I put it?" He rummaged through drawers, pulled files out of cupboards and took down some boxes.

"Ah! Here it is! My Vector 8. No, no that was an old one. Vector 9? No. Vector 15? No. Ah yes, here we are, Vector 77."

Max looked over the Professor's shoulder at a triangular object with sleek fins at the back and a sharp, pointer-like nose.

"It's capable of doing Mach 26, that's twenty-six times the speed of sound," the Professor said proudly. "Of course, there is no sound in space so you wouldn't hear it," he laughed.

"Once you leave the Earth's atmosphere, that's when the rockets kick in. Before that, it takes off like an ordinary plane. It sucks in oxygen directly from the air in order to burn the fuel, and cruises at Mach 2. That's twice the speed of sound," he explained again. "Once it reaches the upper atmosphere where the air is too thin to power the jet engines, the rockets have to take over. They propel the Vector into outer space. From then on it's plain sailing. The higher it gets, the faster it will go."

"That's exactly what I need to get to the Moon," said Max, suitably impressed.

"And why do you want to get to the Moon?" asked Professor Boggle.

"Well, I want to visit the Man in the Moon," replied Max.

The Professor nodded thoughtfully. "I see. What will you do when you meet him?"

"I… I don't know. I just want to see him."

"Well, I don't know about the Man in the Moon. I do know that the Moon is 240,000 miles from Earth. And when you get there, you may find there are only craters and valleys and mountains which look like a face to us. But there are a lot of interesting phenomena which you could explore."

"What are phe-nom-en-a?" asked Max.

"Magical things, things nobody else has ever seen before," said the Professor. "Well, let's get started if you want to go. But first some tea, I think. Let's see what your mother has sent us today. Chocolate? Oh good, triple chocolate! That should give us lots of energy. Come on, Humphrey, your favourite cake."

After tea they left Humphrey to lick all the plates while the Professor and Max went out to the garage. There in a corner stood a large object covered in lots of sheets. The Professor pulled them off one by one sending clouds of dust into the air. Humphrey, who had just then come in, still licking his lips, sneezed violently and ran out again.

"I didn't know you had actually built the Vector," said Max, gazing in amazement at the plane he had just seen in the Professor's drawings.

"Oh yes, many years ago. I named this one The Beagle." The Professor shook his head. "But nobody was interested. They said it would never fly and it would be too expensive and too impractical. So, I stored it away in here. Let's take a look and see what sort of a state she's in."

They opened a door which creaked and fell off in their hands.

"Oh well, it has been a long time," said the Professor.

They went inside the cockpit and looked at the instrument panel. It was very dirty but the Professor wiped it with his handkerchief and flicked a few switches. Suddenly they heard a voice, a slow, even voice.

"Hello, Professor Boggle. Nice to see you again, after all this time."

"What was that?" Max jumped back in fright.

"Oh, you mustn't mind Caracatus," said the Professor. "He's my onboard computer. He's just a bit annoyed that I haven't been to visit him lately."

"A talking computer?" gasped Max. "How did you do that?"

"Oh, it's really quite simple," said the Professor. "You just program the sounds we make into a dictionary that the computer has. I used Humphrey's voice," he whispered. "That's why he sounds so grumpy." He polished a few more switches.

"Let me introduce you. Caracatus, this is Max. He wants to go to the Moon. Max, this is Caracatus.

"Hellooo," said Max, cautiously.

"I am pleased to meet you, Max," said Caracatus in an even, computer-sounding voice.

"Caracatus is a good example of artificial intelligence," said the Professor.

"I beg your pardon," interrupted Caracatus. "Real intelligence, not artificial."

"Yes, yes, Caracatus, we all appreciate how intelligent you are. Now I'm going to try to connect you up again so that you can propel the Beagle for Max and take him to the Moon."

"Oh?" said Caracatus with a question mark in his voice. Then he remembered his manners and said, "I would be delighted", but without much enthusiasm.

"Now mind, I won't say it's going to be easy but we'll certainly have fun trying, won't we, Max?" said the Professor, nodding excitedly.

Max nodded too, but he still couldn't get over the Beagle and Caracatus and the fact that he was standing in a machine that would actually take him to the Moon.

2

Getting Ready

So, every day after school Max hurried to the Professor's house and together they worked on the Beagle. Max helped by cleaning every knob and wire and piece of material – graphite fibre, the Professor called it, a material which was very strong and very light. They looked at maps of the Moon and Professor Boggle told him all about the Moon's features, the mountains and the Rheita Valley, Janssen Crater, and Hadley Rille.

Max would study the maps while the Professor looked over his drawings and changed something here and adjusted something there and made new parts where new parts were needed. He taught Max about flying and what it would feel like in space where there was no gravity to hold you down.

"The spaceship is pressurised so you won't need a space suit inside. But, of course, you'll want to get out and go for a walk on the Moon so you'll need this." And the Professor pulled out from one of his many boxes a shiny silver suit with padded arms and a helmet with a clear window to look out of. "Try it on."

Max climbed into the suit and although he felt a little bit silly, especially when Humphrey started rolling around on the floor laughing, he was starting to feel like a real astronaut.

"Now, this is to help you breathe because there is no oxygen on the Moon and this tube here will…" and the Professor continued to explain all the gadgets and attachments on the suit, which would help Max to walk on the Moon.

Then one day his father met him as he came back late from the Professor's house.

"Where have you been, Max?" he asked.

"At Professor Boggle's."

"And what were you doing there?"

Max did not want his parents to find out that he was getting ready to fly to the Moon.

He was sure that they would try to stop him. He did some quick thinking.

"He's… he's helping me with my… my science project."

"Is that so? Well, I've just received a note from your science teacher who says that you are two weeks late with your science project. Now, I don't want you to go to Professor Boggle's anymore until you've finished all your homework. You are spending too much time messing about at his house and not enough time on your work."

"But Dad…!"

"No buts, Max. I'm doing this for your own good. Now go to your room, please, and start your homework. I'll phone the Professor and tell him that you're not allowed to come over for a while."

Max went up to his room feeling very sorry for himself. He knew his father was right and he should have kept up with his homework but he really, really wanted to go to the Moon. And besides, what he was learning from Professor Boggle was a lot more interesting than some boring old science project.

He sat at his desk and got out his homework. "What is the most interesting body in our universe?" was the question.

"The Moon, of course," he sighed. But he'd never get there. Not now. He looked again at the drawings the Professor had given him and all the notes they had made. This was the ignition button and here was the fuel gauge and there was the directional control system.

And if you switched this lever to automatic, then Caracatus would take over and fly the spacecraft.

Max decided to have just one more look at the Beagle. And then he would do his homework. He waited until his parents had gone to bed and then crept quietly down the stairs and out the back door. He ran down the street to the Professor's house and slid into the garage.

Max went up to the spacecraft. It looked so impressive, all shiny and ready to go. He would take just one look and then go back home. He climbed into the cockpit. He looked at the control panel and pointed to each switch trying to remember what it did.

Ignition, fuel gauge, directional control.

"Arrggghhh, wee-owww," said a voice behind him.

Max jumped, frightened by the sudden sound. As he did so, his elbow knocked the ignition switch. With a roar, the engines started and to his surprise, the garage doors opened!

3

Up, Up and Away

"What's going on?" cried Max. He wondered if it was all a bad dream – the sort you have when you're in a spaceship that's about to take off.

Humphrey stretched and yawned. He had been fast asleep on the back seat. "Oh, it's you. It's a new device the Professor put in. When you start up the Beagle, the garage doors open automatically. To let you get away as quickly as possible."

"Humphrey! Help me! What am I supposed to do now?" shouted Max as the Beagle rolled out of the garage.

"I don't know," said Humphrey sleepily. "I'm just a cat. Ask Caracatus."

Max flicked the switch, which allowed him to talk to the in-flight computer.

Caracatus' light came on. "Ignition on. Engines on. Garage doors open. Further instructions, please."

The spaceship continued to roll down the lawn gathering speed.

"Tell him where you want to go," said Humphrey from the back seat. Max looked out the window as the Beagle raced down the street. Soon they would be coming to his house.

"Ah, ah, to the Moon? I guess," he said softly.

"Louder, please" said Caracatus.

"To the Moon!"

"Are you sure?" asked Caracatus.

"Yes."

"Are you really sure?"

Max took a deep breath. "Yes, I'm really sure."

"Does your mother know you're doing this?"

"Just go, Caracatus," said Humphrey, "so I can finally get some sleep."

"Message received."

Max watched as the nose of the Beagle lifted off the ground and the spacecraft shot straight up into the air. His house was a very small dot below.

"We are climbing to 100,000 feet," reported Caracatus. "Do you wish to continue?"

Max thought for a moment, watching his house and town disappear underneath him.

There was no turning back now. "Yes," he said, "please continue, Caracatus."

"Message received. We will soon be leaving the Earth's atmosphere at 17,000 miles per hour."

As they moved higher and higher, Max could see how beautiful his planet was. He could make out green forests and brown fields and yellow deserts and blue oceans and mountains and rivers and lakes. Soon they were flying over the Great Wall of China.

"This is better than a geography lesson!" he said excitedly.

Suddenly Caracatus' voice interrupted his thoughts. "We have a problem."

"Oh, now what?" growled Humphrey, still half asleep.

"I have only been programmed to leave the Earth's atmosphere. Jet fuel is low.

Instructions, please."

"Well, Max," said Humphrey, "this is your trip. What do you want to do?" He yawned. "I want to get back to sleep."

Max thought back to the charts and diagrams he and the Professor had poured over.

Once the Beagle reached the upper atmosphere – the stratosphere - the rockets would take over and he could shut down the jet engines. Then the Beagle would be propelled into outer space and the higher they went, the faster they would go because there was no gravity in space. Nothing to hold them back.

But he had to find the right switch and only he could decide when it would be the right moment to shut down the jet engines and start the rockets. Not much pressure then?

"Caracatus, what is our position, please?"

"Height: 60,000 feet. Distance from Moon: 240,000 miles."

"Speed?"

"We are travelling at Mach 2 and slowing to 1,000 miles per hour."

This was the right moment.

"Shut down engines, please. Fire rockets one and two."

"Shutting down jet engines." Then, "Engines shut down," reported Caracatus.

There was silence. Not a sound could be heard.

"Rocket one fired. Rocket two fired."

Suddenly a "whoosh!" sound shook the spacecraft and threw Max back into his seat and Humphrey against the roof.

"Hey!" shouted Humphrey, "Can't a cat get some peace around here?"

The Beagle sped off into space leaving the Earth behind. All around them was blackness and night. Soon they could make out millions of stars and the Milky Way.

Ahead of them they could see an – asteroid?

"Oh, oh, this could be tricky, Caracatus," said Max. "Try to steer around that asteroid. We don't want one of those rocks hitting the Beagle and damaging it." *Or us*, he thought.

"I am aware of the danger," said Caracatus. "We will be flying well above it."

"Good work, Caracatus. Set course for the Moon."

"Message received. Setting course for the Moon. But may I remind you," said Caracatus, "that it's cold up there. Have you packed some warm clothes?"

"No," said Max, looking around, "but somewhere in here must be my spacesuit. Yes, here it is. This should keep me warm."

"I'm hungry," came a voice from the back seat and Humphrey raised his head. "Where's my milk?"

"I don't think we've packed any milk, Humphrey," said Max. "The Professor didn't think you'd be coming along. But let me see what we've got in our storage cupboards."

"Storage cupboards? What do you mean? Where am I? Oh no, I'm in a, on a – good grief! We're on a spaceship!"

"Yes, Humphrey, don't you remember? You were asleep on the back seat of the Beagle when I came in."

"Don't – don't tell me! We're not in space, are we?"

"Yes, Humphrey. We're in space."

"Oh no, I thought it was a dream! A nightmare!"

"It's not a dream, Humphrey. We're going to the Moon. Aren't you excited?"

Max could tell that Humphrey wasn't. "To the Moon?" shrieked Humphrey. "I can't go to the Moon. I'm a cat. Cats don't go to the Moon. Let me off! I want to get off!"

Max did some quick thinking. The last thing he needed in space was a panicking cat.

"Humphrey, what do you like most in the world?"

"Why mice, of course. There are some nice mice in Professor Boggle's garage. And that's where I should be."

"But there are even more mice on the Moon," said Max.

"What? What do you mean, 'mice on the Moon'?" asked Humphrey suspiciously.

"Why everyone knows that the Moon is made of green cheese. And you know that mice like cheese. So, don't you think that a place that is made of cheese would attract lots and lots of mice?"

"Well, that's true," said Humphrey, smacking his lips. He could go for a mouse right now, or maybe even two. "Okay, let's go. How much further?"

"Caracatus, please report position."

"We are currently twenty miles from the Moon. To starboard."

"Good, that's where the Sea of Tranquility is. A perfect place to land. Please set course for the Sea of Tranquility, Caracatus. We will land there."

"Message received."

Max and Humphrey looked out of their windows at the large, grey dusty object below.

Coming up fast was a deep, dark valley. Max kept his hands on the controls in case Caracatus needed help landing the spacecraft. It would be tricky. They had to judge the distance just right and land the Beagle carefully so as not to damage the landing gear. If they hit a rock or got stuck, it would be almost impossible to lift off again.

"Caracatus," said Max, looking out the window for signs of a safe landing spot, "slow rocket engines, please."

"Message received. Speed at 50 mph."

Then Max saw it. A large flat area in a valley surrounded by grey mountains. No rocks in sight. This would be the perfect place to land the Beagle.

"Caracatus, shut rockets off. Engage landing gear. Ease her down, please."

"Message received. Landing gear engaged."

They heard the engines shut down. It was very still and the spacecraft seemed to be floating slowly, slowly down to the surface of the Moon.

"Slowly, Caracatus," said Max. "Nice and easy."

Suddenly there was a major wobble and the spacecraft rocked back and forth.

"He said, 'nice and easy'!" shouted Humphrey.

"Sorry," said Caracatus. "It is my first time."

"That's alright," said Max, gripping the controls. "I've got the wheel. I can steady her."

They saw the ground approaching and with the smallest of wobbles, they touched down.

The Beagle had landed.

"We've done it!" Max called out. "Humphrey, we've done it! We made it to the Moon!"

"Excuse me," coughed Caracatus, "but I think I helped a little."

"Of course, you did," said Max, patting the computer. "We couldn't have done it without you."

"Where's my mouse?" said Humphrey. "Let's get out there and catch some mice!"

"Well, Humphrey," said Max, thinking quickly. "We'll have to put on our spacesuits. There's no oxygen on the moon so we won't be able to breathe without one."

"Spacesuit? What spacesuit? I don't have a spacesuit?"

"Well, in that case," continued Max, "you'll just have to stay here." He zipped himself into his suit. "I'm going outside to have a look around. But if I see a mouse, I'll be sure to bring you one."

Humphrey wasn't happy but there was nothing he could do. So, he grumbled again and curled up on the back seat.

4

Interesting Phe-nom-en-a

Max opened the hatch and lowered the ladder. A little cloud of dust spurted upwards. He climbed down carefully and jumped the last few steps.

"Humphrey, Caracatus, can you hear me?" Max spoke into his transmitter. "That was a small step but it really seemed like a giant leap. There is so little gravity here." He could see Humphrey at the window waving his paw and nodding at him.

He took a few more steps. It was very dusty, almost like fine sand and he had to move slowly. But he couldn't resist trying a little jump just to see what it felt like. Whoops!

He seemed to be flying over the surface and landed several feet further on. He would have to be a little more careful if he didn't want to lose his balance. But still, it was fun!

He took a good look around. In the distance he could make out some mountains. Those must be the Mountains of the Moon, and over there was the Hadley Rille canyon. So that had to be the Torres Littoral Valley over there. But everything looked cold and grey and, well, dead.

He turned to the right and saw something rising above the horizon. It was blue and white and as it slowly got larger, he realised it was his own planet, Earth. He was amazed how beautiful it looked, especially compared to the Moon.

Humphrey was waving from the window of the spacecraft and pointing. He was getting quite agitated and Max thought he must be hungry and wanting a mouse. But then he looked to where Humphrey was pointing with his little furry paw. What Max saw nearly made him jump out of his spacesuit!

Four creatures were peeking out from behind a huge rock a few feet away. Max couldn't tell if they were humans or animals or – oh no! – aliens! He had never seen any aliens before so he didn't really know what to expect. Perhaps they were friendly.

On the other hand, what if they weren't? Maybe he should get back to his spacecraft as quickly as possible.

Before Max could make up his mind, one of the aliens waved to him and came out from behind his rock. He was covered in a greyish, greenish, shiny material and Max couldn't tell whether it was his skin or whether he was wearing a spacesuit. The alien had a large head and huge, bulging eyes but he was smiling.

He bounced up to Max and, pointing to himself, said, "Oog!"

Max wondered if maybe this was a greeting. Or maybe the creature was introducing himself? So, pointing to himself, he said, "Max. My name is Max. How do you do?"

"Hoooww dddooo youuu dddooo?" repeated the alien. He jumped up and down smiling. He waved at his companions to come over. The other three bounced out from behind the rock. One of them was carrying a box with an antenna. They all looked greyish-greenish as well, except for one who had green spots and the littlest who was green all over.

Oog introduced his three companions: Zoog, who was carrying the box with the antenna, Moog who was covered in green spots and Oogli Woogli who must have been Oog's son, because he was very small and kept trying to hide behind him! The other aliens were all about Max's size and were waving and pointing and speaking in a language that Max couldn't understand.

"Hoooww dddooo youuu dddooo?" they each said in turn and Zoog held the box up to Max and turned some dials.

"Please repeat."

Max was astonished but repeated slowly, "How do you do? Suddenly he heard the box speak in a voice which sounded very much like Caracatus except higher and more like a girl's.

"We welcome you. Where do you come from?"

Max was more amazed than ever but he figured out that this must be a box, which translated their language into his and his language into theirs. That was the only way that made sense. And it was seriously weird.

"Thank you," said Max. "I come from over there," pointing to the blue planet, "from Earth."

There was excited chattering when the box translated this piece of information.

"This is very good! We have been studying your planet. Come with us and see."

They all took hold of Max and led him over to the large rock. He turned around to see Humphrey looking very worried but Max wasn't frightened. These seemed like very nice aliens.

When they arrived, Max could see that his new friends had a huge telescope which they wanted him to look through. He bent down and was surprised to see his town and just off to the left was his house! He moved the eye-piece a bit more and there was Professor Boggle's house and there was the Professor looking up and down the street!

Oh dear, he must be wondering what had happened to the Beagle. And to Caracatus. And to Humphrey.

"Oh, I can see Professor Boggle!" exclaimed Max. "He is the person who built the spaceship," he explained.

"Professsssooor Boooogggell," they all repeated and Max let them take a look.

"My house is to the left," he said and they looked to the left and looked at Max and said something to the box.

"It must be a very nice place to live."

"Yes," nodded Max. "It is nice," and suddenly he thought of his mother and father and hoped that they hadn't found out he was gone and were worrying about him.

Moog looked at Max and said something to the box. "You must be very homesick to be so far away from home," it translated. And, it was true, Max was beginning to feel just a little bit homesick.

"May we see your spaceship?" asked Oog.

"Of course, follow me," said Max and he led the way back to the Beagle.

As soon as he opened the door, Humphrey darted into a corner.

"Come on out, Humphrey, and meet my new friends," laughed Max. "This is Humphrey," he explained to the aliens.

"Do, do they have any mice?" asked Humphrey, poking his head out carefully.

The box was translating. "What is 'mice'?" asked Oog. "What is a 'Humphrey'?"

"Humphrey is a cat. A cat that talks. Not all cats do. But Professor Boggle trained him. And mice are what Humphrey likes to eat," continued Max.

Oogli Woogli went over to Humphrey who was about the same size as him and poked at him curiously. Humphrey growled and Oogli Woogli ran back to his father and hid behind him.

Max scolded Humphrey for frightening the little alien but all the others were laughing, even Oogli Woogli.

"Here, Humphrey," said Oog, "here is something to eat." He pulled out a small tube and held it out to Humphrey. The cat came running up and sucked on the tube.

"Delicious," he purred. "It tastes like dried mice!"

"You must meet Caracatus," said Max and he turned on the computer. "Caracatus, these are my friends, Oog, Moog, Zoog, Oogli Woogli and," he didn't know what to call it, "the box."

Caracatus said very clearly, "Welcome to the Beagle. I am Caracatus, the on-board computer. I am pleased to meet you."

The box was silent for a moment and then began to whirr noisily. It also made a very sweet tinkling sound. Strangely, so did Caracatus. The two computers seemed to be talking to each other.

Zoog tapped the computer impatiently and the box translated for them what Caracatus had said. They all laughed and Oog said something the box obviously didn't want to translate. Zoog tapped again and the box said to Max, "We are happy to meet Caracatus and," it added in a shy little voice, "I think he is very cute."

The aliens had a good look around the spaceship, pointing at this, "oohhing" at that, giggling at something else.

"Where do you live?" asked Max.

"We live in Mars," said Oog.

"On Mars!" shouted Max. "Are you Martians?"

"Yes, but we live in Mars not on Mars. It is very cold on the surface of our planet so we live in underground cities. You must come and visit us. It is not as beautiful as your Earth but it is home."

"Thank you," said Max, "maybe one day I will."

"We must go back now," said Moog, "or we'll be late for dinner."

"Here," said Oogli Woogli shyly, handing Max some rocks, "these are for you." The rocks glinted and twinkled.

"They are Moon rocks, crystal rocks," said Oog. "They are as old as your Earth – four and a half billion years old."

"Oh!" said Max and Humphrey in amazement. "Thank you very much. Professor Boggle will be really excited about this."

Max looked around for something to give them. The Professor always kept a fresh flower in the spacecraft because he knew Caracatus liked flowers.

"Here," he said. "This is a rose. It grows on Earth. I hope you like it."

"Thank you very much!" Oog, Zoog, Moog and Oogli Woogli said together. They waved as they climbed out of the spacecraft. "Goodbye! Get home safely. Take good care of your planet. It is very beautiful."

5

Heading Home

Max and Humphrey watched as the aliens jumped into the air and bounced over the rock they had been hiding behind. They collected their telescope and bounced away into the distance in the direction of the Rheita Valley.

"They must have their spaceship there," said Max. "I wish I'd asked to see it."

"Well, maybe next time," said Humphrey. "But don't you think we'd better be getting back, too?"

"You're right," said Max. "We don't want the Professor to worry – or my parents," he added. He took one last look around. He could see the grey desert landscape of craters and the tops of volcanoes that he hadn't had a chance to explore. Maybe, as Humphrey had said, next time. Over the horizon he could see the Earth as a large blue and white ball. It really was a very beautiful, a very special place.

Maybe you had to get away from somewhere to really appreciate it.

"Fire up the rockets, Caracatus, please," said Max as he shut the hatch. "We're going home."

"Message received," said Caracatus. "Excuse me, Max," he added.

"Yes, Caracatus?"

"Did you get the number of that little translator box? She really made my circuits crackle."

Max laughed. "I'm sure she'll be in touch, Caracatus."

The rockets fired and they lifted off from the surface of the Moon kicking up a cloud of dust behind them. Soon they were out in the darkness of space. Stars, comets and asteroids were all around but ahead of them was their planet guiding them home.

They had a pretty good flight back. They nearly had a collision with a meteorite but Caracatus and Max managed to avoid it in time.

As they landed the Beagle in Professor Boggle's yard, the sun was just beginning to come up over the horizon and the Moon was fading into the sky. Professor Boggle was looking out his window and rushed down to meet them.

"Hello, Professor!" shouted Max and Humphrey excitedly. "We've been to the Moon!"

"We brought you back some Moon rocks," said Max, "and we met some really nice aliens from Mars."

"And I ate dried mice," said Humphrey, "but I'm really hungry for a fresh one!" and he ran off into the garden.

"So you made it, Max, you made it to the Moon!" cried out the Professor who still couldn't believe his ears.

"Yes, Professor, we made it! Thanks to you!" nodded Max. "But I'll tell you all about it later. I've got to get home now before my parents wake up and miss me."

And Max ran home, let himself into the house very quietly and climbed into bed still thinking of his wonderful adventure.

The next thing he knew, his mother was shaking him gently and saying, "Max, dear, wake up. You'll be late for school. My goodness, you must have been having a good dream. You were miles away," she laughed.

"You've no idea, Mum," Max managed to say.

"Have you been working on your science project? What planet are you going to write about?"

"The Earth," said Max. "It is the most important, and," he added, hugging himself, "the most beautiful."